3 —

Y0-CAF-580

As Fans of 3, this book is dedicated to the three people whose unconditional love and support continue to give me steadfast belief that anything is possible...thanks to my mom, dad, and wife.

In loving memory of Nanaji...

www.mascotbooks.com

Through the Eyes of Om: Exploring Malaysia

©2019 Sonny Tannan. All Rights Reserved. No part of this publication may be reproduced, stored in a retrieval system or transmitted in any form by any means electronic, mechanical, or photocopying, recording or otherwise without the permission of the author.

For more information, please contact:
Mascot Books
620 Herndon Parkway #320
Herndon, VA 20170
info@mascotbooks.com

Library of Congress Control Number: 2018908399

CPSIA Code: PRT1018A
ISBN-13: 978-1-64307-219-7

Printed in the United States

THROUGH THE EYES OF OM:
Exploring Malaysia

Written by
Sonny Tannan

Illustrated by
Agus Prajogo

My name is Om, and I'm going to take my first airplane ride!

Can you tell how excited I am? I get the chance to visit Malaysia, the country my mommy is from. I will also get to meet some very special people for the very first time!

Have you ever been on an airplane before? Do you remember where you went on your first plane ride?

I am a bit nervous. Planes are big, and I don't know anything about where I'm going. Traveling from Baltimore, Maryland, to Malaysia will take a long time! The good news is that there will be family all around me to make sure I am comfortable and welcome wherever I go.

BALTIMORE

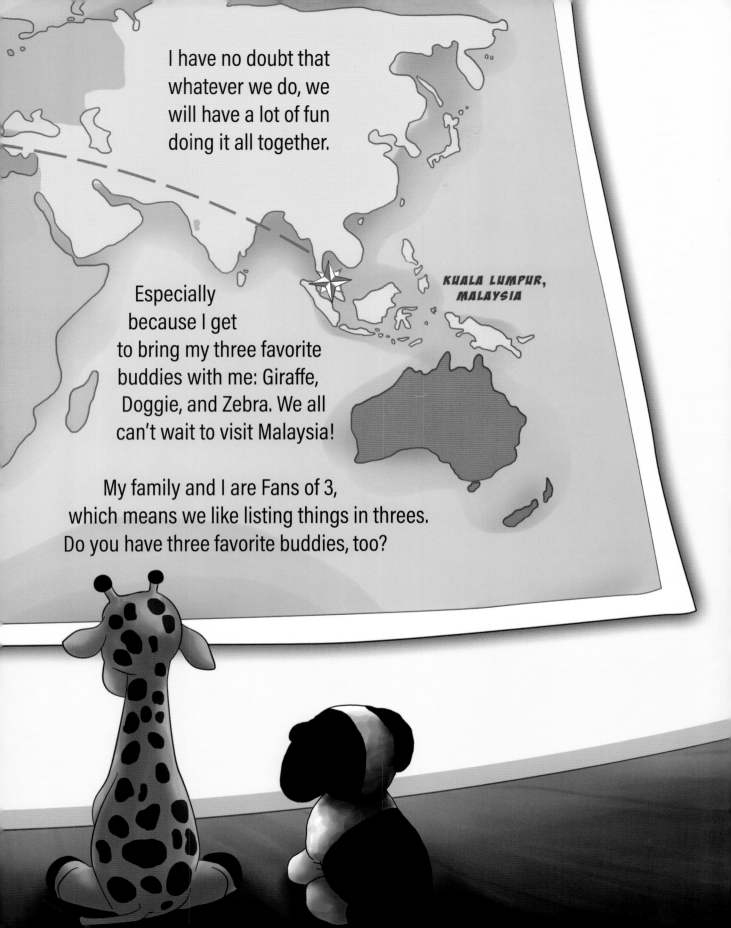

I have no doubt that whatever we do, we will have a lot of fun doing it all together.

KUALA LUMPUR, MALAYSIA

Especially because I get to bring my three favorite buddies with me: Giraffe, Doggie, and Zebra. We all can't wait to visit Malaysia!

My family and I are Fans of 3, which means we like listing things in threes. Do you have three favorite buddies, too?

First things first...I can't go on a trip without packing my bags. Luckily, my mommy and daddy will make sure I have the right clothes, nappies, and plenty of snacks for the airplane ride. With their help, I get to choose some books, crayons, and toys to bring with me. It's going to be a loonnnggg ride!

Mommy and Daddy told me some fun facts about Malaysia. Here are my three favorites:

- The tallest twin buildings in the world are the Petronas Towers in Kuala Lumpur. They are each 1,483 feet high. That's a little taller than nine football fields stacked on top of each other!
- There are thousands of *hawker centres* throughout Malaysia. They sell yummy foods and juices. I hope I have enough time to try them all!
- It takes nearly 270 steps to climb up to the main attraction and view of the skyline of the city center at the Batu Caves. Guess who wants to make it all the way to the top?!

The day finally arrived. We were about to leave for Malaysia!
We took an Uber to the airport, went through security, and
sat at our gate before we boarded the plane. The
plane was so big, and I got a seat all to myself!
We buckled our seatbelts, the plane
started to taxi...and then we took off!

I remembered how scared I thought I would be, but it turns out it wasn't scary at all. Malaysia, here we come!

We flew and flew and flew...the flight lasted almost 22 hours!

The big moment had finally arrived, and we landed at the Kuala Lumpur airport. I was going to meet some of my family members for the first time!

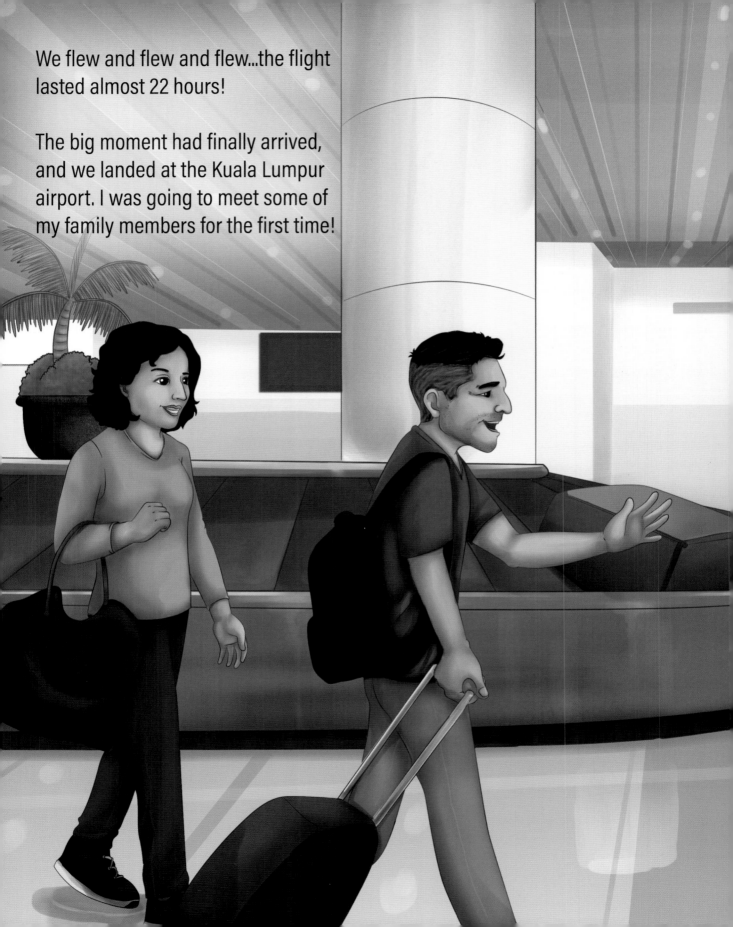

When we were waiting to pick up our suitcases, I heard some voices saying, "Om, Om...over here!"

There were my *Naniji* and *Nanaji* waving at me with big smiles on their faces! My mommy and daddy told me that those were my grandparents, and that they were waiting to meet me. I ran as quickly as I could to give them a big hug and kiss.

M A L A

PERLIS

KEDAH

PENANG

KELANTAN

PERAK

TERENGGANU

PANGKOR
ISLAND

SELANGOR

PAHANG

KUALA
LUMPUR

MELAKA

JOHOR

N

W   E

S

After we picked up our suitcases, we all headed to Naniji and Nanaji's house to meet the rest of my family. When we walked to the car, I noticed how hot and humid it was. Mommy told me that this was because Kuala Lumpur is located just above the equator. I was so happy we brought sunnies, flip flops, and shorts!

Once we arrived at their house, I met lots of uncles, aunties, and cousins! But the most important person that I wanted to meet first was my *Bibiji*, also known as my great-grandmother. I was taught the importance of paying my respects to my elders...and my Bibiji was the eldest.

Did you know that my Bibiji has lived for a long time? She is 91 years old! I was a bit nervous to meet her for the first time. What does a 91-year-old great-grandmother look like? Would she like me? Would I like her? What do you think happened when I saw her for the first time?

When I met her for that first time, she smiled at me and I wasn't scared anymore. In fact, I ran up to her and gave her a hug.

She gave me lots of kisses and some special gifts. In fact, let me share three things that I learned in terms of how to show respect to my elders.

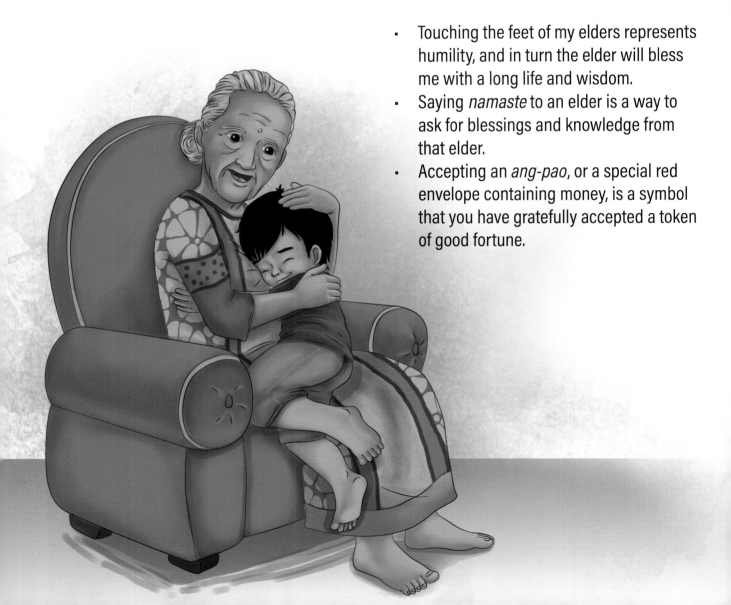

- Touching the feet of my elders represents humility, and in turn the elder will bless me with a long life and wisdom.
- Saying *namaste* to an elder is a way to ask for blessings and knowledge from that elder.
- Accepting an *ang-pao*, or a special red envelope containing money, is a symbol that you have gratefully accepted a token of good fortune.

I'm so lucky that I got to meet my great-grandmother!

Next, we needed to get some food because I was hungry!

Here are the three best foods I tried while I was in Malaysia:

- Satay on a stick dipped in a peanut sauce is sooooo yummy. It also happens to be one of my mommy's favorite dishes!
- Roti canai is a fluffy, flaky bread dipped in lentil curry. It makes your hands a bit messy, but my daddy loves eating this dish with me (we try to share!)
- My absolute favorite is Hainanese chicken rice. This is rice with roasted chicken and cucumber with a sweet spicy chili sauce...nom nom!

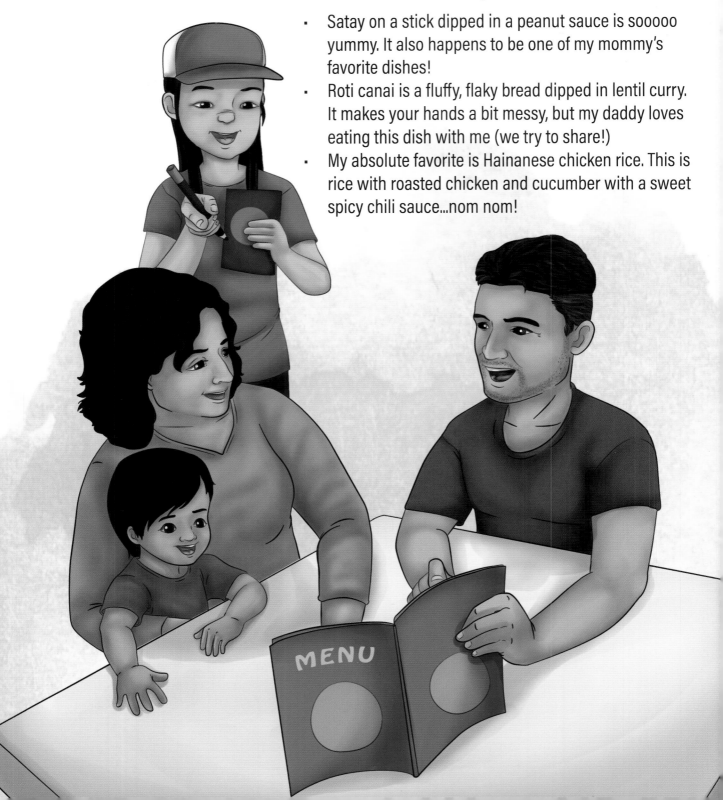

ROTI CANAI

HAINANESE CHICKEN RICE

SATAY

Not only was this my first trip to Malaysia to visit family, but I was also going to get a chance to celebrate my birthday in a different country!

At least fifty of my family members came to celebrate...can you imagine how many presents I got to open at my party? I even received an ang-pao. I wonder how much was in mine?!

We all spent time together and danced the afternoon away...by the end of my party, I wasn't the only one who wanted to take a nap!

But if you ask me, my favorite part about the entire party was getting the chance to meet each and every one of my family members. Because at the end of the day, life is all about spending time with the people you love!

Our trip to Malaysia was coming close to an end, and after two weeks of visiting we had to fly back home. Before we left, I made sure to give plenty of hugs to each of my uncles, aunties, and cousins.

As we got into our car to go to the airport, I waved good-bye to all of them. I was a bit sad that I would be leaving them, but I had a lot of fun with my family in Malaysia and can't wait to visit them again.

As we took off in the airplane to head back home to the United States, I tried to think about all the things that I experienced on my first trip to Malaysia.

Being a Fan of 3, these are the three things I learned while on vacation:

- Family, near or far, is everything.
- I love traveling around the world.
- Malaysia is a wonderful place!

So, the big question I'm sure you are all already thinking about is...where do you think I will travel to next?!

Glossary

Hawker centres: similar to American food trucks, these are mobile stands where a variety of local foods and juices are sold

Naniji: grandmother

Nanaji: grandfather

Bibiji: great-grandmother

Namaste: a respectful greeting with hands clasped in front of you in a prayer style as you speak

Ang-pao: special red envelope that contains money given as a gift

About the Author

Who is Om? He's a cheeky young boy that loves to travel and explore the world. As Fans of 3, his adventures usually include three of his favorite observations or life lessons. You can follow along on his LinkedIn video channel which he first started in 2017.

Om's daddy Sonny is a United States Marine Corps veteran who has always had a passion for giving back—not only to his country, but to his community. From the moment he brought Om home from the hospital, they have been best friends.

Om and Sonny love hearing what kids and adults think of their stories. If you have an idea for a future project, feel free to connect with them on LinkedIn, Instagram, or Facebook. You can also check out their webpage and drop them a personal email!
eyesofom3@gmail.com

Have a book idea?

Contact us at:

info@mascotbooks.com | www.mascotbooks.com